THE PATIO CLUB®

WRITTEN AND ILLUSTRATED BY
CARYN MOTTILLA

August and Allen

August and Allen
The Patio Club ®
Published by Open Window Publishing
Castle Rock, CO

Publisher's Cataloging-in-Publication data

Names: Mottilla, Caryn, author.
Title: August and Allen / by Caryn Mottilla.
Description: First trade paperback original edition. Also available as an ebook. | Castle Rock [Colorado] : Open Window Publishing, 2019. | Series: The Patio Club.
Identifiers: ISBN 978-0-9997471-9-3
Subjects: LCSH: Old age—Fiction. | Month of August—Fiction. | Aging parents—Fiction. | Short stories.
BISAC: FICTION / General.
Classification: LCC PS374.O43 | DDC 813–dc22

Cover design by Caryn Mottilla

QUANTITY PURCHASES: Schools, companies, professional groups, clubs, and other organizations may qualify for special terms when ordering quantities of this title. For information, email ThePatioClub@gmail.com.

OPEN WINDOW
PUBLISHING

The Patio Club® is dedicated to the men and women in assisted living communities, memory and Hospice care who have listened to the adventures of The Patio Club®. They expressed their hope for these stories to be published and shared with others across the country.

Introducing the Patio Club

The Patio Club was originally formed by two sets of sisters—Elaine and Adele from New Jersey, and Betty and Mildred from Kentucky. The women were young when they met in the 1940s. The years passed by, and later in life, the four adventurous women made a pact that after they died they would meet up and visit retirement and assisted living communities. After they passed away, they came to Happy Visions Retirement Home and liked it so much they decided to stay.

The women call themselves "The Patio Club," because they sit outside on the patio of Happy Visions. Each day, Elaine, Adele,

Betty and Mildred are surrounded by colorful sparkles, and they meet a steady stream of interesting visitors and residents who pass through Happy Visions on their way to unknown destinations.

One amazing thing is that the Patio Club can look to the sky and watch a video of each person's life. This precious gift lets the Patio Club understand the unique story that each person carries with them.

August and Allen

A BOLT OF LIGHTNING LIT UP THE STORMY LATE August sky. It was followed by a crack of thunder so loud even the women of the Patio Club shrieked when they heard it.

All day long, the weatherman had been calling for a storm, yet there was no sign of any truth to that forecast. Right after dinner ended at Happy Visions Retirement Home, coal-black clouds began to form in the sky. It looked like the weatherman was finally going to be right this time.

The women of the Patio Club stood inside of Happy Visions Retirement home watching through the windows as the wind began to blow. Colorful outdoor furniture began sliding across the square stones of the patio. Large, thick raindrops with—some hail mixed in as well—bounced on the ground.

"Look!" Mildred yelled as she pointed to the back yard. Suddenly, a brown and gray hunting dog came running through the bushes. In its mouth, it carried a pheasant. The bird's colorful feathers made it look as though the hunting dog was wearing a mask. The dog slowed down, walked through the wet grass and paused in the yard. The rain made his coat look the color of chocolate.

Elaine, Adele, Betty and Mildred watched in silence as lightning flashed in the distance. In spite of the stormy weather and rain, the dog stood quietly at attention, holding the bird its mouth. He looked to the windows of the residents' rooms as though he were looking for someone in particular.

The wind died down as the storm passed and a soft rain shower fell as the dog continued to wait. Elaine, Adele, Betty and Mildred watched as the dog slowly dropped the pheasant to the ground and sat on the wet grass.

The women of the Patio Club were intrigued by the dog. They quietly opened the screen door and formed a line as they walked in silence over to the dog. Elaine was the first to speak. "Years back, I had an Irish setter named Red. I know this is a hunting dog, but it is not an Irish setter."

Then Betty spoke. "Well, it sure isn't a poodle! We always had poodles when the kids were younger. This dog is definitely a hunting dog. He looks like he's waiting for someone."

Mildred watched the dog with great curiosity. "It looks like it's a short-haired pointer of some sort," said Mildred. "One thing is for sure, he is one heck of a hunting dog to be able to get a pheasant in this storm!"

Elaine slowly approached the dog, patted it on its head and looked at its collar. It was made of old, brown leather with a small, silver plate. Elaine squinted her eyes as she read the engraving aloud to the others. It says "August–Gus."

Betty kneeled on the ground. She spoke kindly to the dog and said, "Well, Gus, we need to get you inside." However, Gus made no attempt to move.

The Patio Club was now surrounded by shimmering green sparkles. The storm clouds were gone, and the darkening sky revealed light from a full moon. The moon's light made the women's sparkles shine even more brightly.

Meanwhile, Gus continued to sit quietly next to the pheasant. In spite of his closed eyes, Gus continued guarding the colorful, lifeless pheasant. Adele had placed a small bowl of water near Gus, but he made no attempt to drink it.

"This dog does not look lost," said Elaine. "It seems as though he is waiting for someone." Suddenly, the women smelled smoke from a cigar. The beautiful dog seemed to smell it, as well. He suddenly opened his eyes and began to wag his tail.

Elaine, Adele, Betty and Mildred followed the smell of the cigar and saw an open window in one of the resident's rooms. The Patio Club knew smoking in the rooms at Happy Visions was not allowed. Cigar smoking was *definitely not allowed*. Betty laughed and said, "Those darn cigar smokers. They never do follow the rules!"

The smell of cigar smoke floated on the evening breeze. Gus sat at attention now and suddenly he barked.

"He must know who is in that room," said Adele. The Patio Club now saw the faint trail of smoke coming through the open window. The women started whispering to each other and went to the open window to catch a glimpse of the cigar-smoking resident.

As the women approached the window and looked inside, they saw a man asleep in a rocking chair. He was wearing a colorful orange robe. The robe looked similar to the color of orange that hunters wear when they are in the woods.

Even though the women continued to smell the cigar, the man was sound asleep in the rocking chair. His eyes were closed and a smile crossed his face. It seemed as though he was dreaming.

"Now I am really curious," said Betty. "This must be his dog. Maybe we should try and sneak Gus into his room through the open window! This seemed like a good idea to the women, but Gus ignored the women even when they used food to encourage him to go inside.

"What are we doing?" asked Elaine. "We should just go sit with Gus and look to the video in the sky to figure out what is going on. The women were fortunate to be able to look to the sky to see each person's story. They sat around Gus on the wet grass. The pale moonlight behind

the video in the sky made it seem as though the small group was watching an outdoor movie.

Elaine started laughing first. "Is it me, or does this remind you of going to those old drive-in movies? That was a long time ago! Good Lord, now we are the old ones!"

As the woman watched the video that played against the navy-blue sky, they saw a man walking through a large field. It was late summer, and the man was smoking a cigar and carrying a hunting rifle. Running beside him was a small puppy. The man began speaking to the puppy as though it understood every word he said.

"Since it's August, I am going to name you after the month and call you 'Gus.' I always want to remember that I found you in August."

"Wait a minute," said Betty. "He looks like the man who is asleep in the rocking chair."

The man in the video continued speaking to the puppy. "If I name you after the month of August maybe that will

help me to remember that's when we first started hunting together. I can tell you my memory won't always be as good as it is now!"

The man brushed the puppy's soft fur and continued to speak to him. "Someday, when I am older, I will live at Happy Visions Retirement Home. When I do, I want you to visit me at night with a bird you found that day."

The women watched the movie in the sky and smiled as the puppy sat listening to the hunter's instructions. "Gus, we won't tell anyone. You will know my room because I will light a cigar. Look for the window with the cigar smoke coming from it! We will probably get into trouble, but it really won't matter. The thing about getting older is you don't worry so much about being in trouble."

Gus sat attentively at the hunter's feet. The young puppy seemed to nod his head, as though signaling to the hunter that he understood.

The video ended as a chill filled the air. Adele noticed the breeze and said, "The smell of the cigar smoke is gone." The four women looked to the old man's room and watched as the light went out. When they looked to the grass, they realized Gus and the lifeless pheasant were gone as well.

"Is anyone else scared?" asked Adele. Upon hearing this, Betty, Mildred and Elaine began to laugh. "Adele, we have sparkles, and we are already dead! Why should we be scared?" All of the women were laughing now. They decided to meet outside the next evening after dinner to see if Gus would return.

The following day, the Patio Club roamed the halls looking for the old man's room. Elaine, Adele, Betty and Mildred found it after lunch. Outside of the room was a glass "memory box." It contained a few photos and a brief description of Allen, the man in the room. The contents of the box remind the staff of Happy Visions of something personal about the person they care for in that particular room.

The Patio Club looked through the items in Allen's glass-covered memory box. He was born in Alabama. Allen had never married. Someone had written on an index card that Allen had loved three things in life. He loved good cigars, hunting and he loved his beloved hunting dog named Gus.

In the box was a newspaper clipping Elaine now read to the others. "Listen to this," said Elaine. "The article said Allen lived in a small house on the edge of town in the mountains. He wrote a column about hunting for the local newspaper. When Gus ran off a few years back, Allen wrote in his column, 'I know wherever Gus is, he will come visit me in my dreams and bring me pheasants!'"

When the women looked in the room, they saw Allen sitting in his rocking chair as he looked through the open window. Betty said, "Allen doesn't have a cigar, but I swear I can smell one!"

As the women turned to leave, Allen softly whispered. As Elaine, Adele, Betty and Mildred listened more closely, they heard Allen say, "Come find me, Gus, it's August!"

"No wonder," said Betty. "It *IS* August!" The women quietly left Allen's room and went outside to wait for evening to fall. They sat quietly on the patio near Allen's open window watching for any sign of Gus.

After sunset, as the moon rose in the sky, Elaine was the first to hear a rustling sound in the bushes near the patio. "Look," Elaine excitedly said as she pointed. Suddenly, Gus came through a leaf-filled opening. He was carrying a pheasant just like he had done the evening before. The pheasant's colorful feathers made Gus look as though he was wearing a mask for a party.

The women watched as Gus quietly sat down. His nose twitched as the smell of cigar smoke filled the evening air. The women of the Patio club looked to Allen's window. Gus' ears suddenly perked up and all of them heard Allen say, "Come find me, Gus. It's August."

Gus ran to the open window with his brown-gray tail wagging. He stood up on his hind legs and looked inside at Allen. Gus barked softly as if answering Allen, and then Gus was gone.

The video in the sky came to life as Elaine, Adele, Betty and Mildred looked at each other. They watched as Gus ran up to Allen's window and barked—then the lights in Allen's room went dark.

Suddenly, the video stopped playing. As the women watched, Allen and Gus ran through the grass outside of Allen's room. Allen now wore his orange hunting vest. Gus was ahead of him sniffing the ground as Allen said, "I knew you would come find me, Gus! It's August!"

This August, may you go hunting, just like Allen and Gus, for something amazing to happen each day.

With love from The Patio Club,

The End.

The Patio Club's Story

IN NOVEMBER OF 2016, I began writing fictional stories for retirement and assisted living communities. This occurred because of a simple request from an older gentleman in his 80s who asked if I could write a story about people "their age." Writing and telling stories has always come easily to me. I happily said , "yes." I was excited at the challenge and have written a story each month since then. They are about a fictional retirement/assisted living community named *Happy Visions*. Each month I read to retirement and assisted living communities. The joy of doing this is overwhelming.

In July of 2017, I was reading to a group of older women as they sat outside *on the patio* in the shade. The women's ages reached up to 95. When I left the patio that day, I decided at that moment to write a story for them called "The Patio Club." The series began with that story.

The stories I write come effortlessly to me. It is as if I am divinely inspired. As I began writing the first story in the Patio Club series, I was so surprised as I watched the story come to life. It is the story of two sets of sisters, Elaine and Adele from New Jersey, and Mildred and Betty from Kentucky. They made a pact that when they died they would meet up and visit retirement and assisted living communities.

Imagine my surprise—because in real life Elaine and Adele (sisters) were my aunts from New Jersey, and Betty (my mother) and Mildred (my aunt) were sisters from Kentucky! My Aunt Mildred was the last one to join The Patio Club. She passed away earlier in 2017. The Patio Club™ stories now touch people from around the country and hopefully someday from around the world.

My dream is that The Patio Club™ series will be read to the people in assisted living, memory and Hospice care communities. As I read each month to these special people, I realized that it is often difficult to visit loved ones who are in the assisted living population. What I have found is that reading a story seems to transform everyone from the reader to the listener. I have seen people with all kinds of health challenges perk up when listening to the joyful adventures of The Patio Club™. They are in the present moment as they listen and during that time there is nothing wrong with them.

My wish is that people will take the adventure of reading a story (about 12 to 15 minutes) from The Patio Club Series to a loved one. It will transform the visit from one where it may be difficult to find something to talk about, to one where both the reader and listener are moved beyond words.

With gratitude and love,

- Caryn

Acknowledgments

THE PATIO CLUB is dedicated to my aunts Elaine, Adele, Mildred, and my mother Betty. Although the characters in the Patio Club are fictional, they are based on these important women who impacted my life.

Special thanks to my sons Carson and Cooper, as well as, family and friends who have listened to these stories. They have enthusiastically cheered for me to follow my dream to write and illustrate stories that bring joy and adventure to the lives of others.

Finally, I am grateful to God for the gifts He has given me to serve the people in assisted living, memory and Hospice care.

About the Author

CARYN BEGAN WRITING children's stories for her children in the 1990s. In 2016, as she read children's stories to assisted living communities, residents asked her to write a story "for people their age." That was how the adventure of writing for the adult and assisted population began.

Since that time, Caryn has written a monthly series called The Patio Club®. It takes place at a retirement home/assisted living community named Happy Visions.

The Patio Club™ are the first stories published by Caryn for that age group. The stories have captured the attention of people of all ages across the country.

The Patio Club™ stories are a bridge between the reader and the listener. Family and friends that visit assisted living, memory and Hospice care communities may struggle for something to talk about. Reading a story like The Patio Club™ to these special residents takes them on an adventure without them ever having to leave the room. It creates an opening for some interesting conversations!

Caryn lives in Colorado. She has two grown sons, Carson and Cooper

www.ingramcontent.com/pod-product-compliance
Lightning Source LLC
Chambersburg PA
CBHW041610120626
46551CB00002B/381